STOOOOOOOOOOOP!

Okay, darlings. Before you turn the page,
let me preface this by saying that
what you are about to see
isn't entirely my fault.

Now, I know this looks bad,
but let a girl explain.

Naughty MAAAABELL!!!
SEES IT ALL

Nathan Lane & Devlin Elliott
Illustrated by Dan Krall

Simon & Schuster Books for Young Readers
New York   London   Toronto   Sydney   New Delhi

For Justin Chanda, who definitely sees it all
—N. L. & D. E.

For Rachel and Mia
—D. K.

SIMON & SCHUSTER BOOKS FOR YOUNG READERS
An imprint of Simon & Schuster Children's Publishing Division
1230 Avenue of the Americas, New York, New York 10020
Text copyright © 2016 by Nathan Lane and Devlin Elliott • Illustrations copyright © 2016 by Dan Krall
SIMON & SCHUSTER BOOKS FOR YOUNG READERS is a trademark of Simon & Schuster, Inc.
For information about special discounts for bulk purchases, please contact Simon & Schuster Special Sales
at 1-866-506-1949 or business@simonandschuster.com.
The Simon & Schuster Speakers Bureau can bring authors to your live event. For more information or to book an event,
contact the Simon & Schuster Speakers Bureau at 1-866-248-3049 or visit our website at www.simonspeakers.com.
Book design by Lizzy Bromley • The text for this book was set in ITC Berkeley Oldstyle.
The illustrations for this book were rendered in Photoshop. • Manufactured in China
0716 SCP • First Edition • 10 9 8 7 6 5 4 3 2 1
Library of Congress Cataloging-in-Publication Data
Names: Lane, Nathan, 1956- author. | Elliott, Devlin, author. | Krall, Dan, illustrator.
Title: Naughty Mabel sees it all / Nathan Lane and Devlin Elliott ; pictures by Dan Krall.
Description: New York : Simon & Schuster Books for Young Readers, [2016] | Summary: "Mabel the naughty French bulldog from the Hamptons gets up
to more hijinks as she takes on 'monsters,' but are they real or does she need to get her eyes checked"— Provided by publisher.
Identifiers: LCCN 2015030001| ISBN 9781481430241 (hardcover) | ISBN 9781481430258 (ebook)
Subjects: | CYAC: Dogs—Fiction. | Behavior—Fiction. | Vision—Fiction. | Hamptons (N.Y.)—Fiction. | Humorous stories.
Classification: LCC PZ7.1.L33 Nax 2016 | DDC [E]—dc23 LC record available at http://lccn.loc.gov/2015030001

But where are my manners?

Hello, my little darlings.
It's me again, Naughty Mabel.
We had so much fun the first time,
I thought a second date was worth a try.

It all began a few days ago when things started to get a little strange around the house.

For some odd reason my doggy dish was filled with potpourri. It actually tasted better than my kibble, but my stomach didn't agree.

However, it did improve my breath.

Even my gas smelled a little better.

Still, the next day I was not only feeling queasy, I was seeing two of everything.

Two front doors, two mothers, two fathers—it was too too much.

And then I was watching Martha Stewart on television and saw THREE of her making couscous, which made me faint.

No more potpourri for me!
I was just about to say something
to my parents when I got the most
exciting news.

I'd been invited to my first sleepover at Smarty-Cat and Scaredy-Cat's house.

A SLEEPOVER, PEOPLE! I mean, how adult! How divine! I'm a strong, independent girl! I was ready to venture out into the world and take a big bite out of it!

Finally I knew how rock stars must feel.
How on earth does one choose what to bring?

Easy! Just take everything.

My parents said it was only for one night and that I shouldn't get too excited. *Please*, have we met? It's like they don't know me at all!

For the record, Smarty-Cat and Scaredy-Cat's mother is more than just a nice, old lady who lives next door.

Her name is Millicent Murgatroyd. As a young woman she was an aviatrix (a female pilot who flies airplanes—thanks, Google!),

a paleontologist (digging up bones— we have a lot in common),

and a university professor of history and anthropology! Smell her.

One day she found a large shoebox on her front doorstep. Inside there were two kittens— one very nervous, the other smart as a whip—and they grew up to be my BFFs!

The evening started very well. Smarty and Scaredy
and I were having a great time playing dress-up.

Then we settled in to watch one of Millicent's old black-and-white movies. Not my idea of an exciting way to end the night, but what are you going to do? She's 70. That's 490 in dog years.

I got bored and dozed off. I didn't care about Bette Davis or why she had all that makeup on. My own snoring woke me up, and out of the corner of my eye I spotted a mysterious shadow on the wall.

I decided to investigate.

I knew it! It was a little blurry because of the dark, but there was no getting around it. . . .

It was a monster!
Monsters are a tricky
and elusive bunch.
And the room was
crawling with them!

I grabbed the nearest weapon I could find and jumped into action!

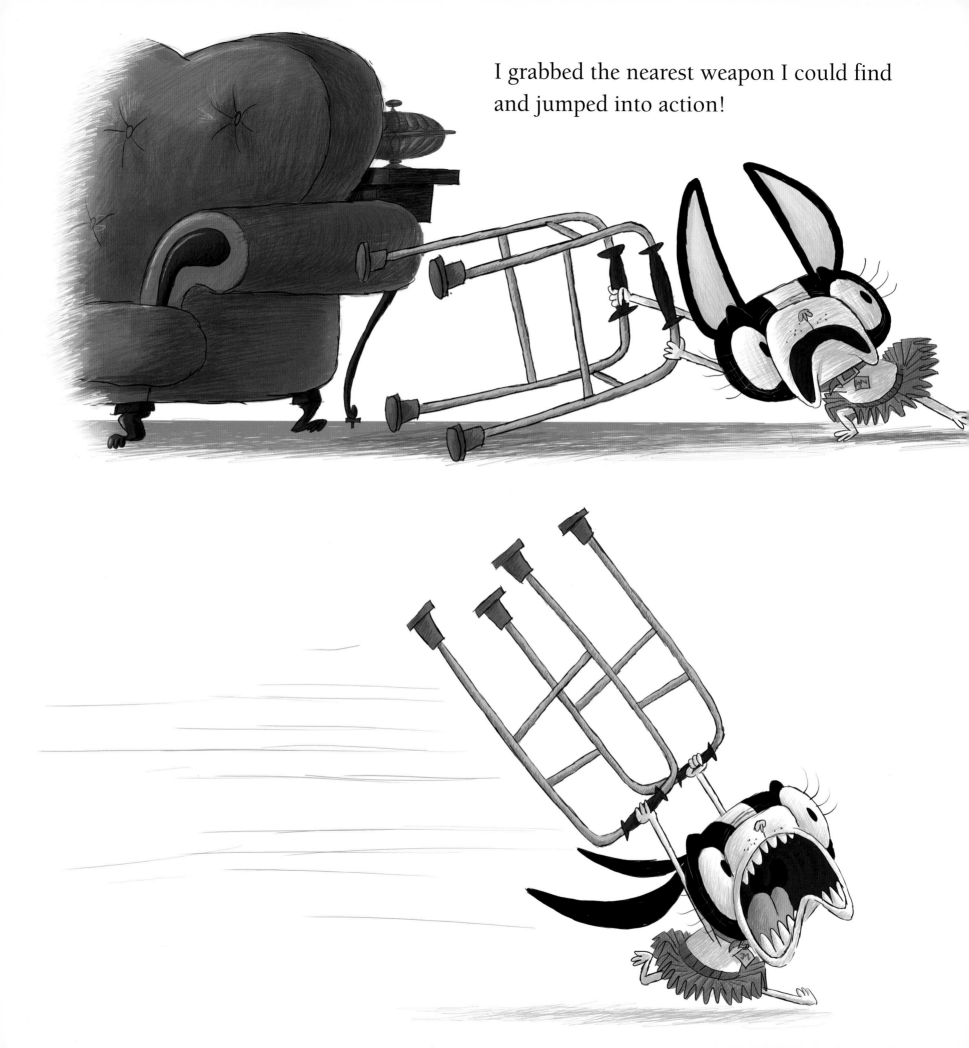

Mrs. Murgatroyd didn't seem to appreciate my heroic efforts. Maybe if she cleaned her house once in a while it wouldn't be infested with monsters . . . but I decided this probably wasn't the best time to bring that up.

Apparently, even my parents don't believe in monsters. Right, and there's no such thing as the Tooth Fairy or the Easter Bunny either.

Some people just can't handle the truth.

Anyway, they just called me naughty and put me to bed.

So demeaning. So confusing. I saved many lives. Maybe next time I'd just let the monsters eat them. Maybe I'd just . . .

But then I saw something!

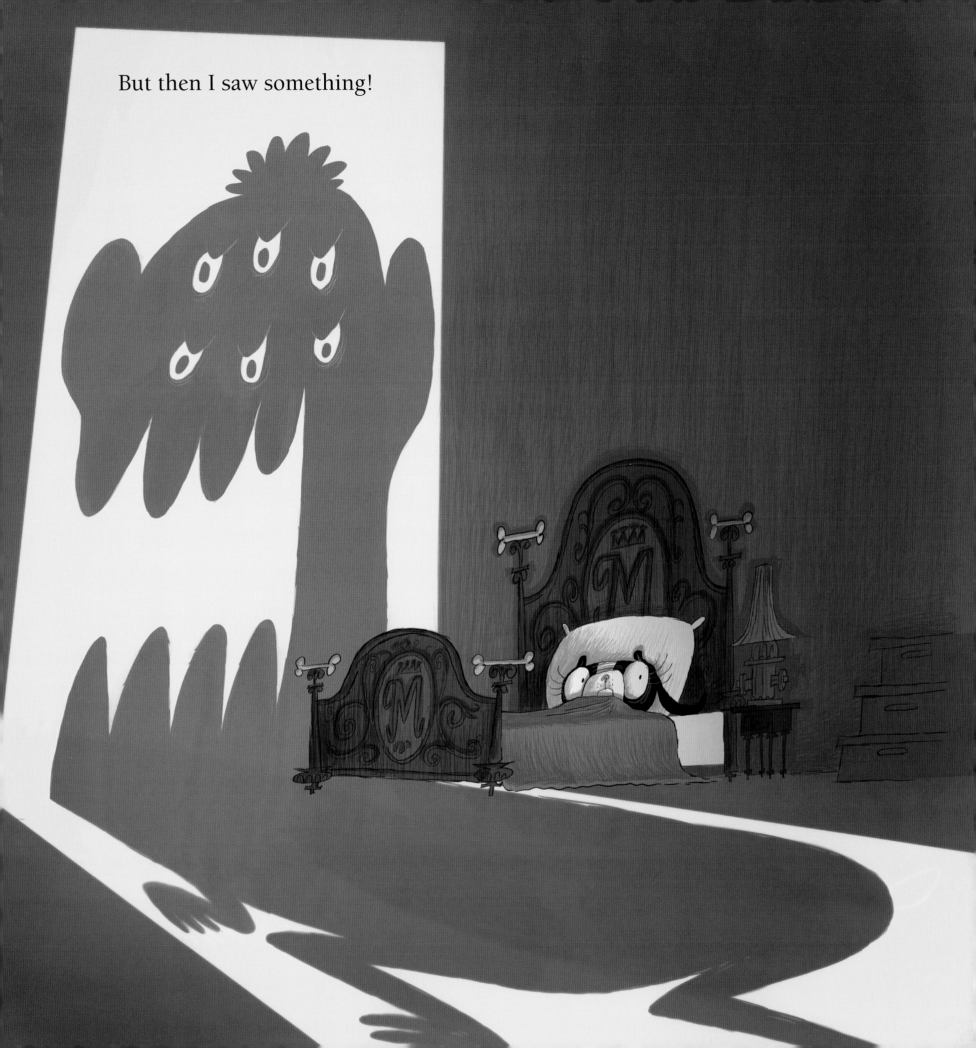

I knew it! The monsters followed me home to have their revenge. Isn't that just like monsters? They like to play with your head.

But if I could catch one, I could prove I was right. And I love being right.

So I called out, "Here monster, monster. Come out, come out, wherever you are." I could play their little game.

And that's when I spotted one! It was huge!
This monster needed to lay off the carbs.
I decided I had to either attack it or wake up
my parents with the good news.

Attaaaaaaaack!!!!!

Can you believe it? My parents still couldn't see the monster.

Now, if you'll recall, this is where we began.
I decided to turn myself in and get time off
for good behavior.

Only I couldn't figure out who to turn myself in to.

They seemed to be cloning! I had no idea which lucky couple were my real parents.

Or what was happening.

Fortunately, the smartest couple figured it out.

Guess what? There were no monsters.
I needed glasses!

Glasses for a dog! Who knew? They had to take me to an optimist, an optopotamus, an op-tha-mo-lo-gist . . . Oh, you know, the eye doctor?

I wasn't sure I liked the looks of the joint.
The room positively reeked of regret.
I swore I'd be good. I'd give up believing in monsters.
I was cured. We could go get smoothies!

Everything looked . . .

ohhhhhh . . .

ahhhhhhhhh . . .

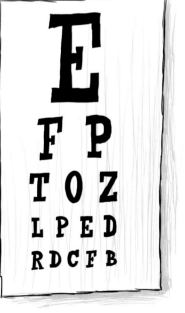

better.

That explained a lot. My bad.

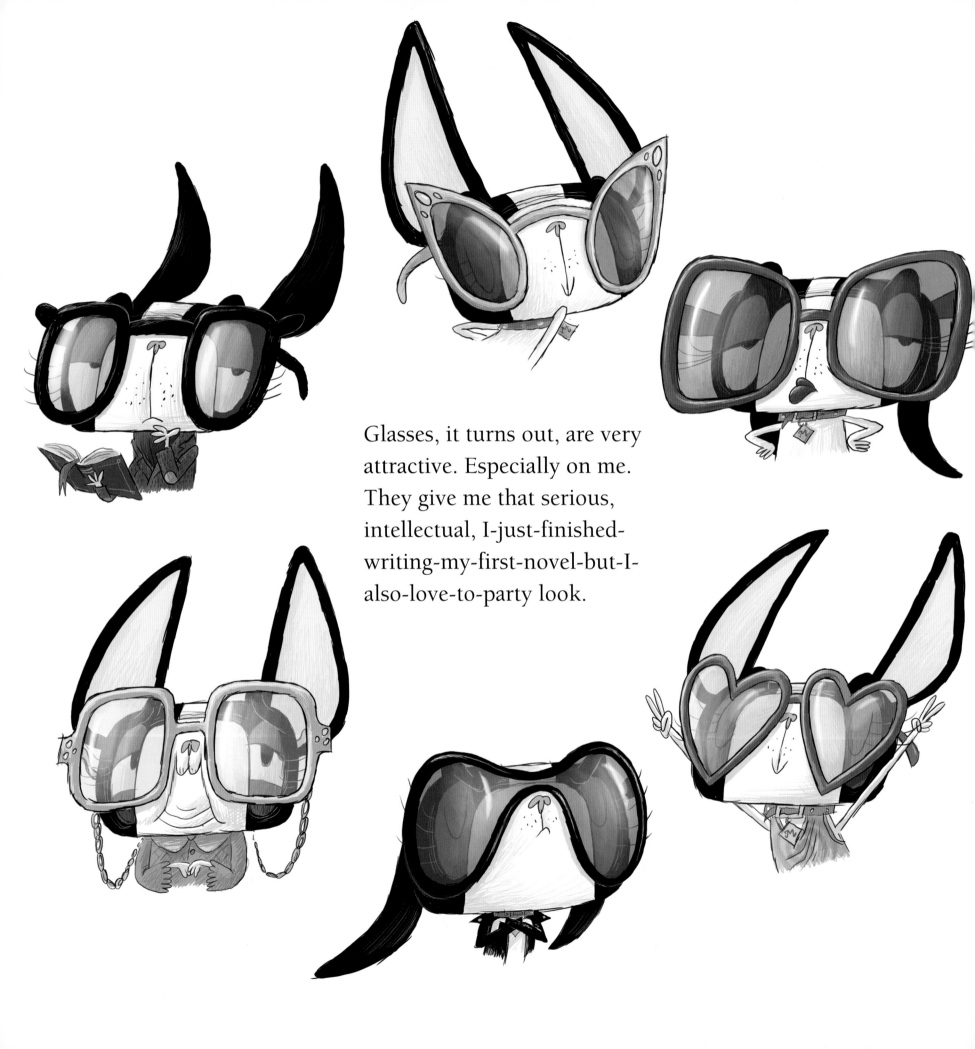

Glasses, it turns out, are very attractive. Especially on me. They give me that serious, intellectual, I-just-finished-writing-my-first-novel-but-I-also-love-to-party look.

Heavens, I thought I heard another monster.
(No one bought that.)

My parents decided contacts would be more practical
for an active girl like me. And they were right as usual.

So what can we learn from all this, darlings?

Well, sleepovers are potentially fraught with danger.

And life is full of surprises . . .

but you can always count on your friends and family
to help you out when you don't see things clearly.

And by seeing things clearly, I mean I see that pile of leaves. I see it's not a monster, so I see no reason to attack.

But where's the fun in that, darlings?